G.I. JOE SIGMA 6

script:
ANDREW DABB

pencils:
CHRIS LIE

inks:
RAMANDA KAMARGA

colors:
ROB RUFFOLO

lettering:
BRIAN J. CROWLEY

editor:
MIKE O'SULLIVAN

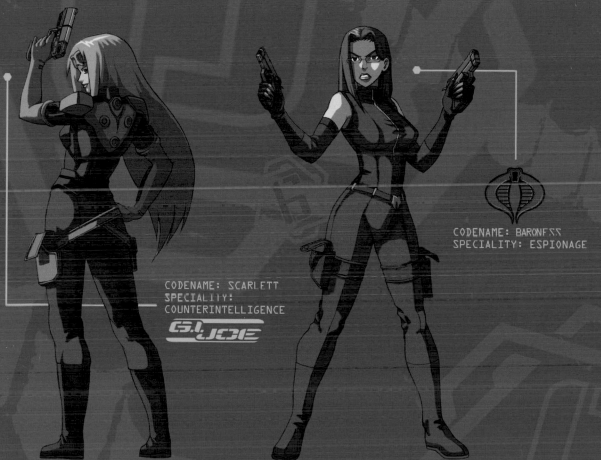

CODENAME: SCARLETT
SPECIALITY: COUNTERINTELLIGENCE
G.I. JOE

CODENAME: BARONESS
SPECIALITY: ESPIONAGE

HIGH FASHION

DDP

Spotlight

visit us at www.abdopublishing.com

Exclusive reinforced library bound edition published in 2008 by Spotlight, a division of ABDO Publishing Group, Edina, Minnesota. This edition is produced under agreement with Devils Due Publishing, Inc. www.devilsdue.net

Library of Congress Cataloging-in-Publication Data

Dabb, Andrew.
    High fashion / script, Andrew Dabb ; pencils, Chris Lie ; inks, Ramanda Kamarga ; colors, Rob Ruffolo ; lettering, Brian J. Crowley ; editor, Mike O'Sullivan. -- Exclusive reinforced library bound ed.
        p. cm. -- (G.I. Joe SIGMA 6)
    Revision of issue 4 (Feb. 2006) of G.I. Joe Sigma 6.
    ISBN-13: 978-1-59961-371-0
    ISBN-10: 1-59961-371-9
        1. Graphic novels. I. Lie, Chris. II. O'Sullivan, Mike. III. G.I. Joe Sigma 6. 4.
IV. Title.

PN6727.D23H54 2008
741.5'973--dc22

                                                                2006052227

All Spotlight books have reinforced library bindings
and are manufactured in the United States of America.

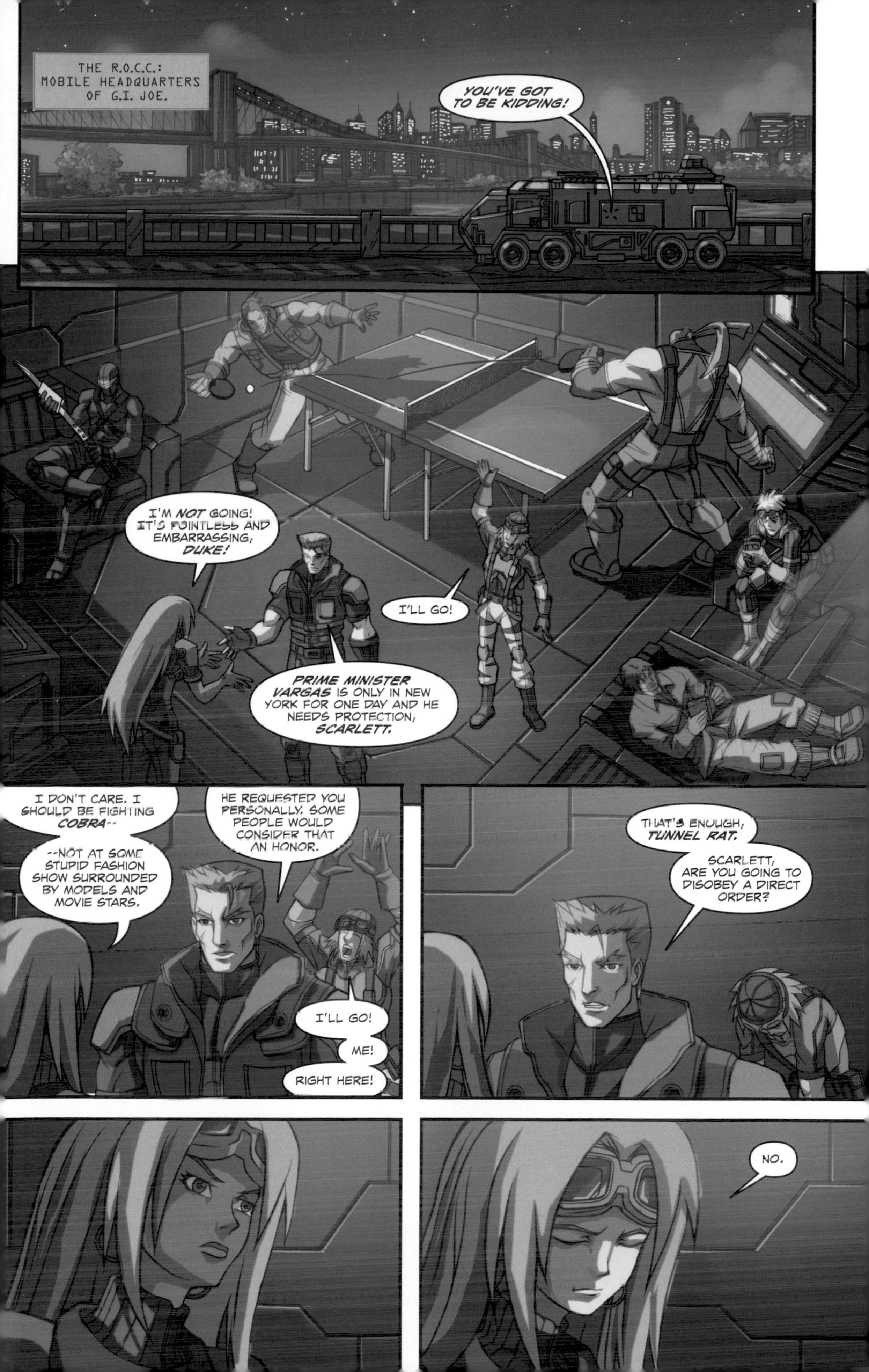
THE R.O.C.C.: MOBILE HEADQUARTERS OF G.I. JOE.
YOU'VE GOT TO BE KIDDING!
I'M NOT GOING! IT'S POINTLESS AND EMBARRASSING, DUKE!
I'LL GO!
PRIME MINISTER VARGAS IS ONLY IN NEW YORK FOR ONE DAY AND HE NEEDS PROTECTION, SCARLETT.
I DON'T CARE. I SHOULD BE FIGHTING COBRA--
--NOT AT SOME STUPID FASHION SHOW SURROUNDED BY MODELS AND MOVIE STARS.
HE REQUESTED YOU PERSONALLY. SOME PEOPLE WOULD CONSIDER THAT AN HONOR.
I'LL GO!
ME!
RIGHT HERE!
THAT'S ENOUGH, TUNNEL RAT.
SCARLETT, ARE YOU GOING TO DISOBEY A DIRECT ORDER?
NO.

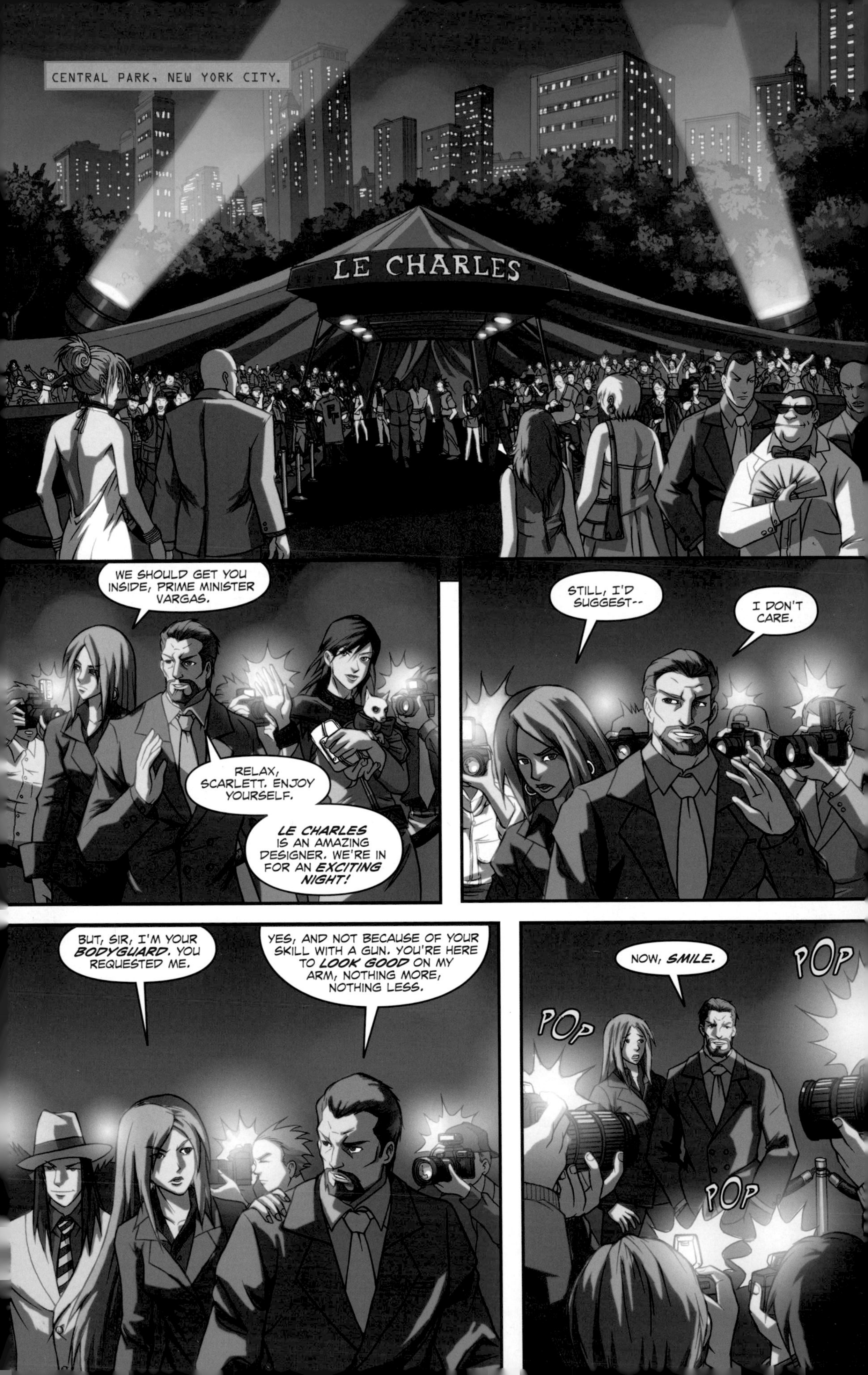
CENTRAL PARK, NEW YORK CITY.
LE CHARLES
WE SHOULD GET YOU INSIDE, PRIME MINISTER VARGAS.
RELAX, SCARLETT. ENJOY YOURSELF.
LE CHARLES IS AN AMAZING DESIGNER. WE'RE IN FOR AN EXCITING NIGHT!
STILL, I'D SUGGEST--
I DON'T CARE.
BUT, SIR, I'M YOUR BODYGUARD. YOU REQUESTED ME.
YES, AND NOT BECAUSE OF YOUR SKILL WITH A GUN. YOU'RE HERE TO LOOK GOOD ON MY ARM, NOTHING MORE, NOTHING LESS.
NOW, SMILE.
POP
POP
POP

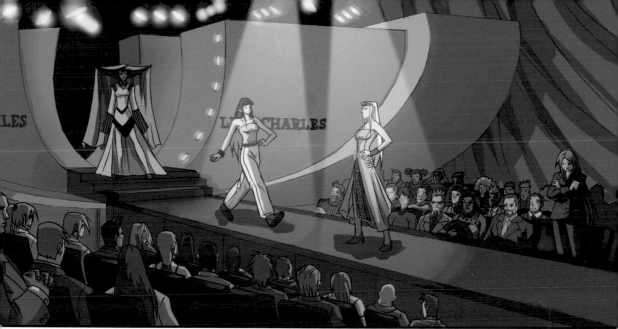

≶SIGH≷

THIS IS *RIDICULOUS*, SCARLETT. PLEASE SIT DOWN.

WHAT'S THE MATTER, I'M NOT LOOKING *GOOD ENOUGH* FOR YOU?

YOU HAVE TO UNDERSTAND, I'M SURE YOU'RE *FAIRLY COMPETENT* WHEN IT COMES TO PERSONAL SECURITY; BUT--

I'M A *LOT MORE* THAN "FAIRLY COMPETENT."

FINE, YOU'RE *LIBERATED* AND *EQUAL* AND AFFIRMATIVE ACTIONED AND ALL THAT. BUT IF I WANTED SOMEONE TO STAND NEXT TO ME AND LOOK *MENACING*, I WOULD HAVE BROUGHT A MAN.

THIS IS AN *ELEGANT* EVENT; I NEEDED A *BEAUTIFUL WOMAN*, AND YOU WERE AVAILABLE; THERE'S NOTHING *INSULTING* ABOUT THAT. IF ANYTHING, IT'S A *COMPLIMENT*.

NOW SIT DOWN.

I'D RATHER NOT.

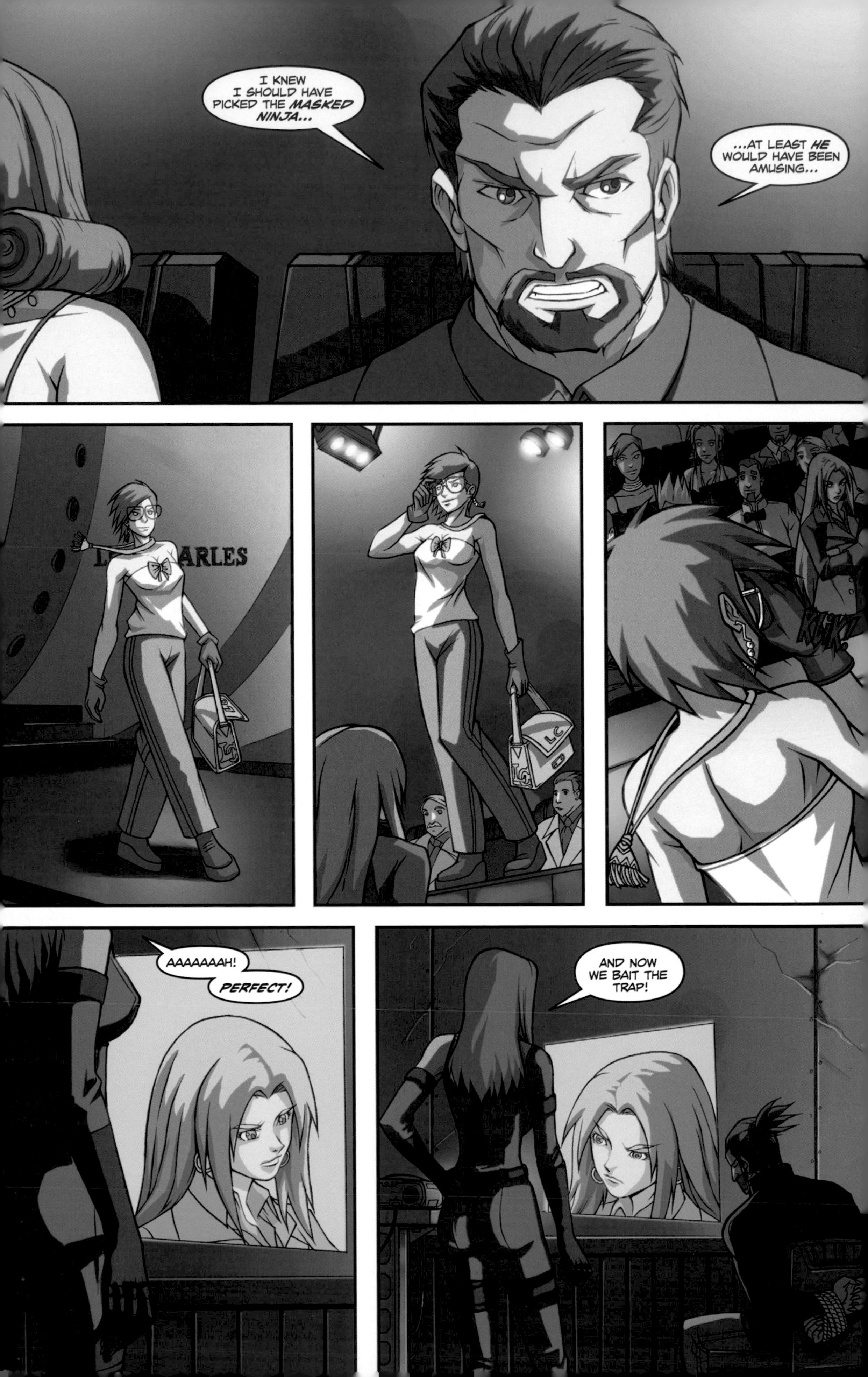
I KNEW I SHOULD HAVE PICKED THE MASKED NINJA...
...AT LEAST HE WOULD HAVE BEEN AMUSING...
AAAAAAAH!
PERFECT!
AND NOW WE BAIT THE TRAP!

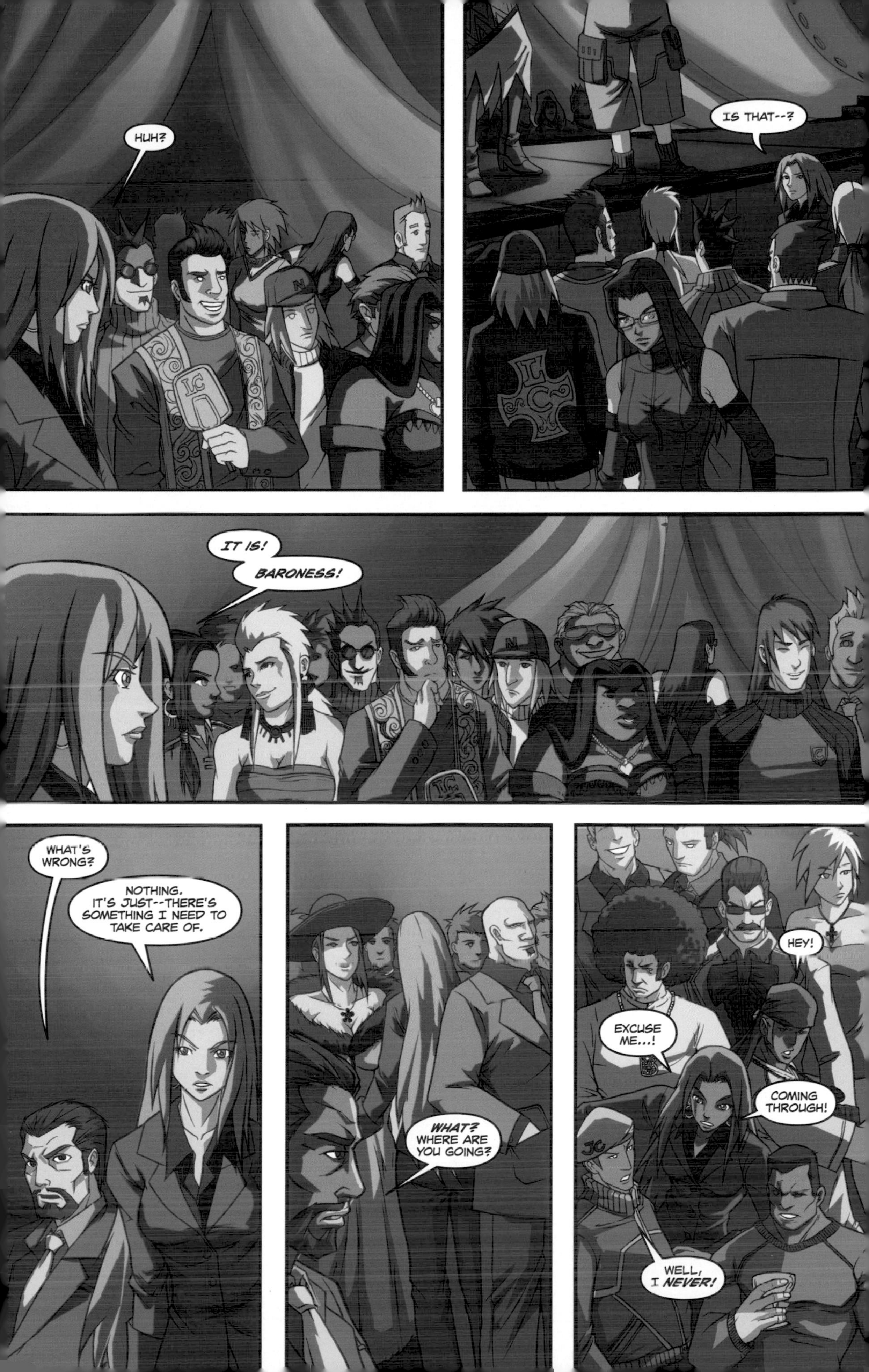
HUH?
IS THAT--?
IT IS!
BARONESS!
WHAT'S WRONG?
NOTHING. IT'S JUST--THERE'S SOMETHING I NEED TO TAKE CARE OF.
WHAT? WHERE ARE YOU GOING?
HEY!
EXCUSE ME...!
COMING THROUGH!
WELL, I NEVER!

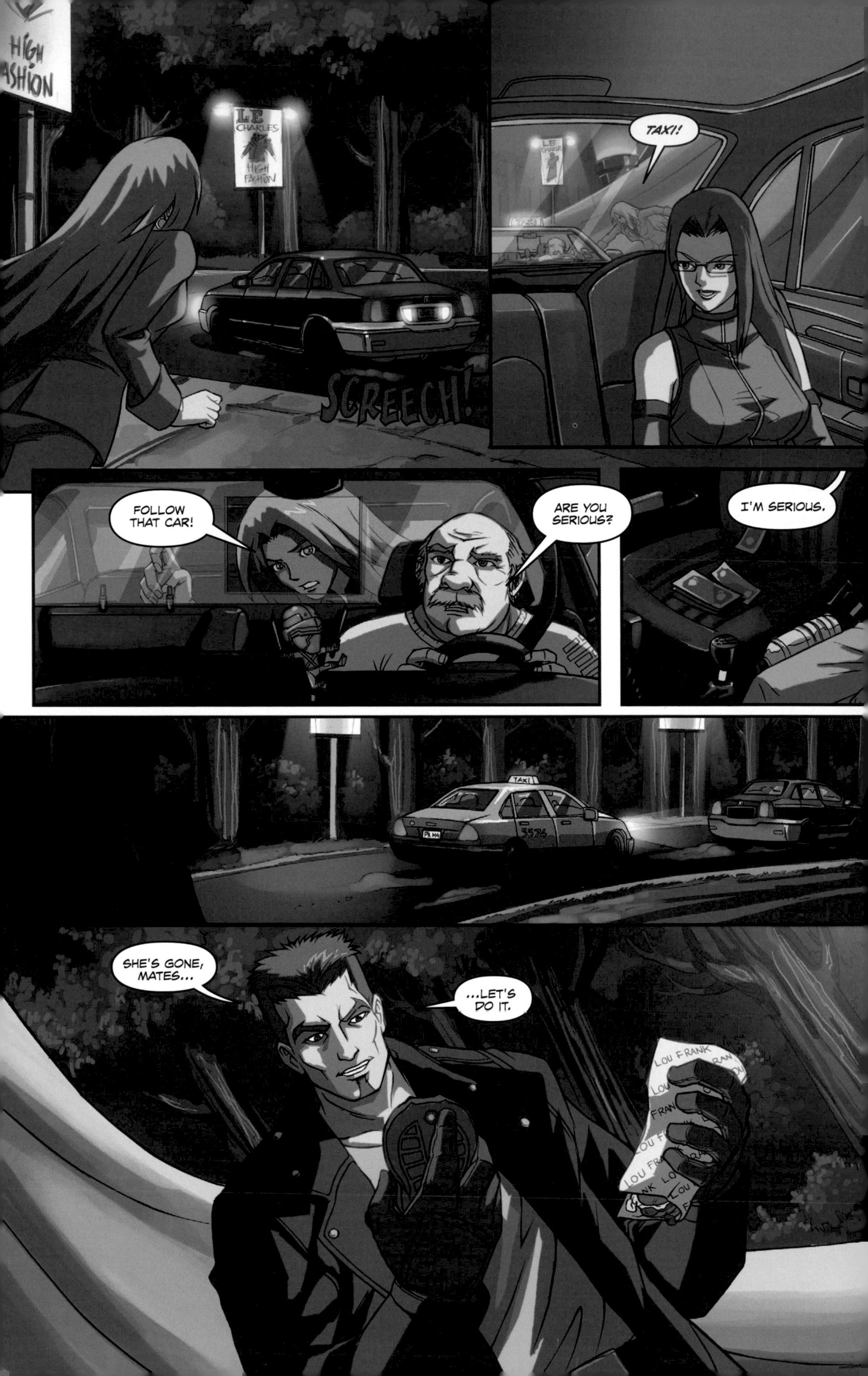
HIGH FASHION
LE CHARLES HIGH FASHION
SCREECH!
TAXI!
FOLLOW THAT CAR!
ARE YOU SERIOUS?
I'M SERIOUS.
TAXI
SHE'S GONE, MATES...
...LET'S DO IT.
LOU FRANK

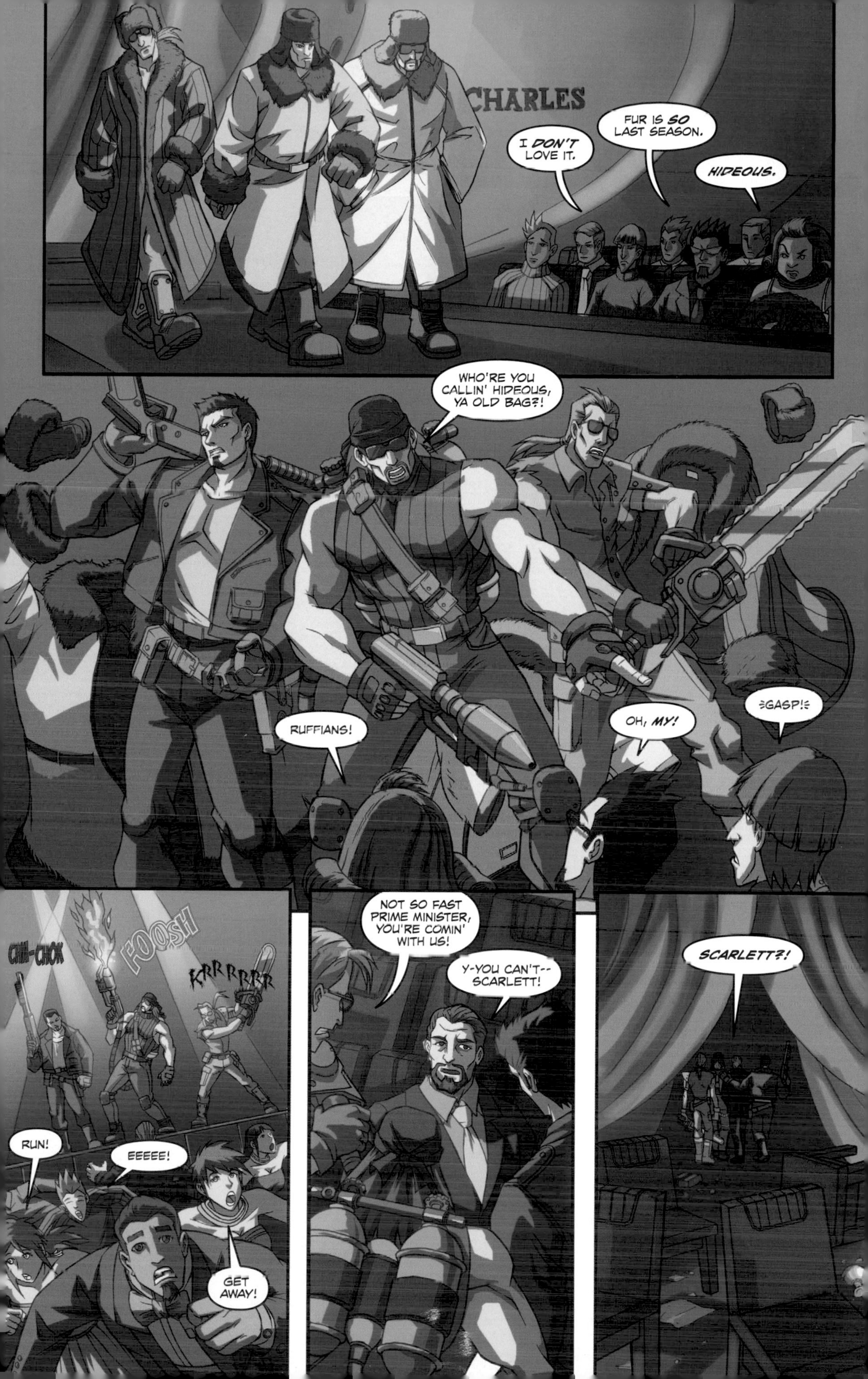
CHARLES
I DON'T LOVE IT.
FUR IS SO LAST SEASON.
HIDEOUS.
WHO'RE YOU CALLIN' HIDEOUS, YA OLD BAG?!
RUFFIANS!
OH, MY!
GASP!
CHI-CHOK
FOOSH
KRRRRRR
RUN!
EEEEE!
GET AWAY!
NOT SO FAST PRIME MINISTER, YOU'RE COMIN' WITH US!
Y-YOU CAN'T-- SCARLETT!
SCARLETT?!

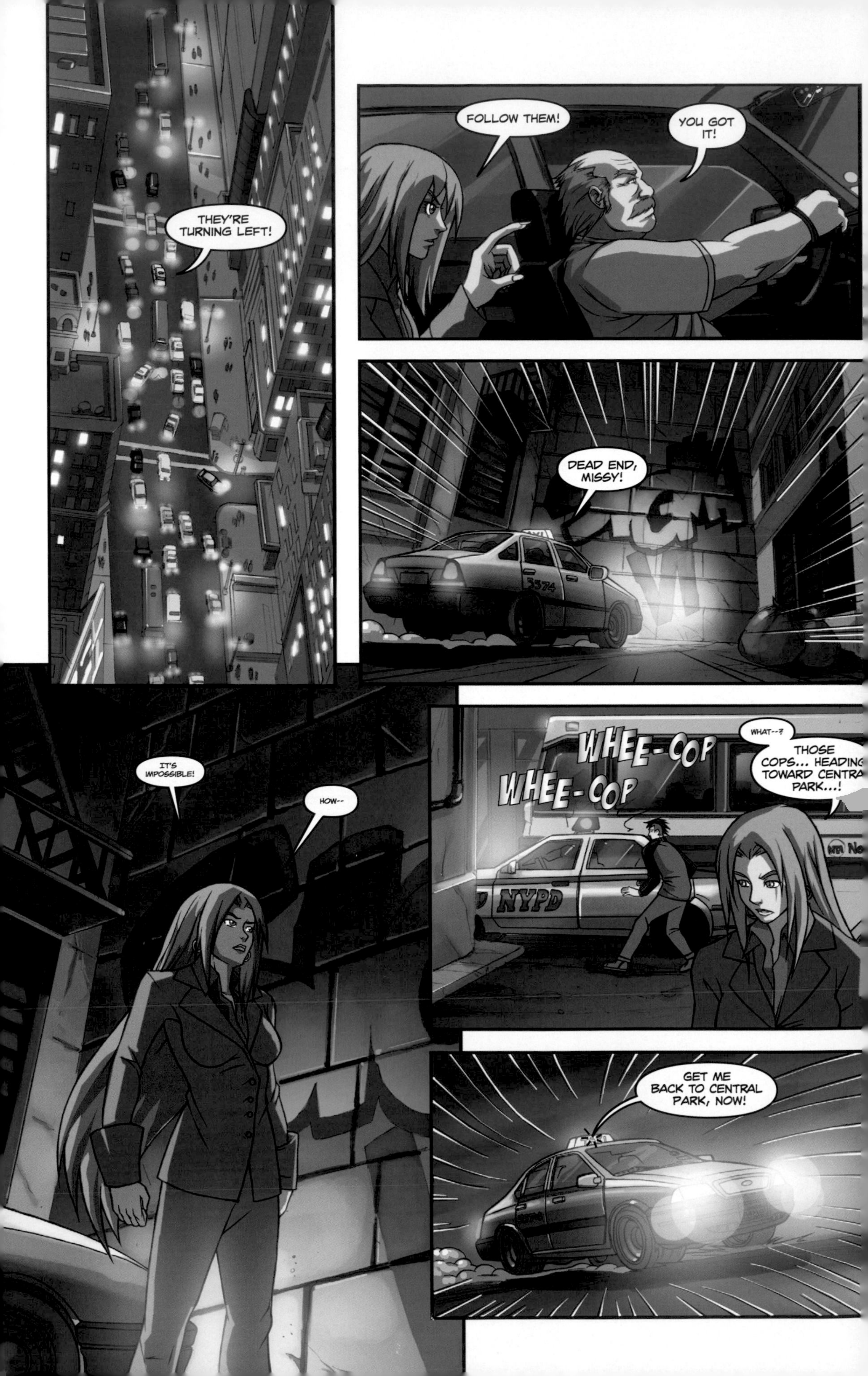
THEY'RE TURNING LEFT!
FOLLOW THEM!
YOU GOT IT!
DEAD END, MISSY!
IT'S IMPOSSIBLE!
HOW--
WHEE-COP
WHEE-COP
WHAT--?
THOSE COPS... HEADING TOWARD CENTRA PARK...!
GET ME BACK TO CENTRAL PARK, NOW!

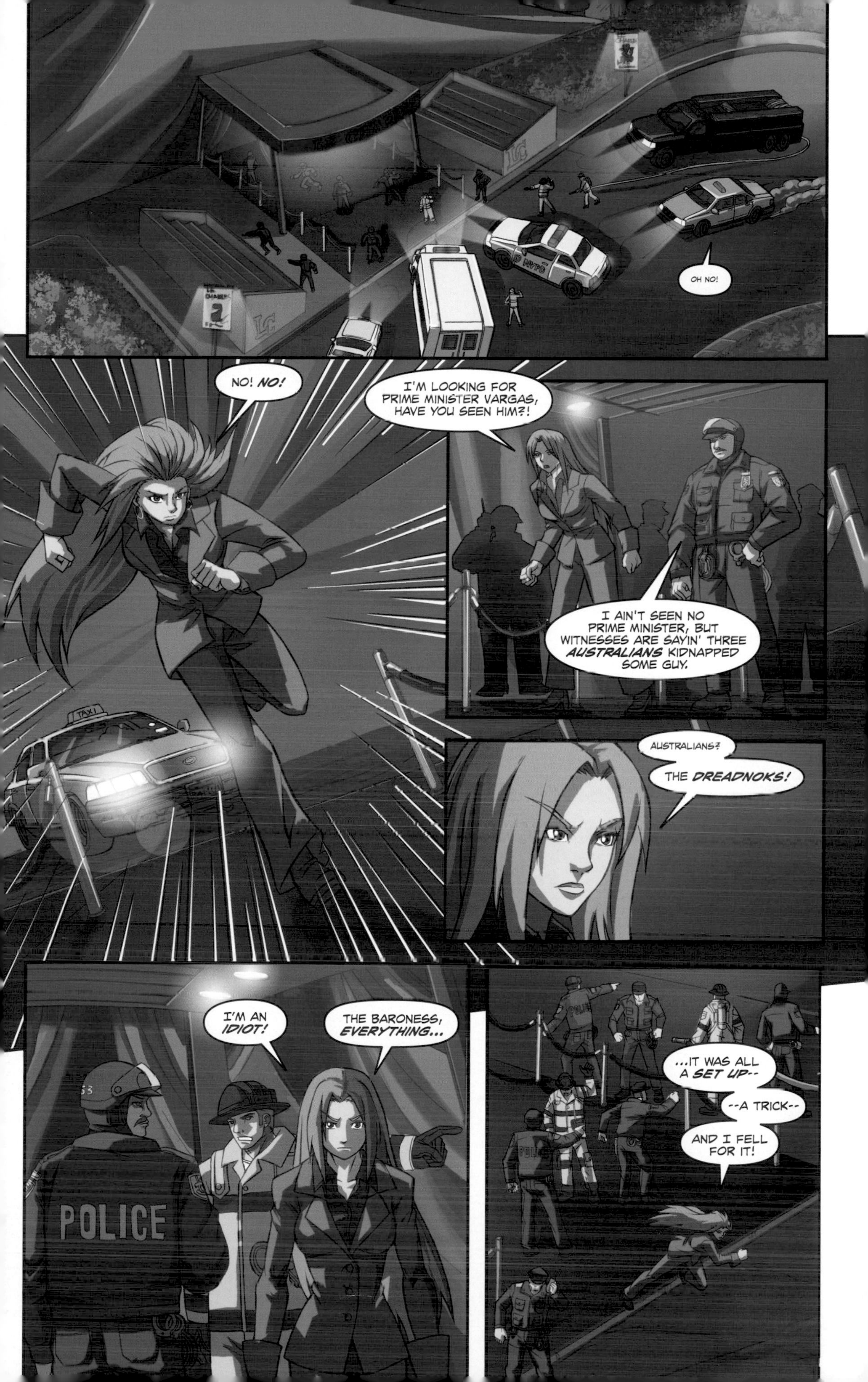
OH NO!
NO! NO!
I'M LOOKING FOR PRIME MINISTER VARGAS, HAVE YOU SEEN HIM?!
I AIN'T SEEN NO PRIME MINISTER, BUT WITNESSES ARE SAYIN' THREE AUSTRALIANS KIDNAPPED SOME GUY.
AUSTRALIANS?
THE DREADNOKS!
I'M AN IDIOT!
THE BARONESS, EVERYTHING...
...IT WAS ALL A SET UP--
--A TRICK--
AND I FELL FOR IT!
POLICE

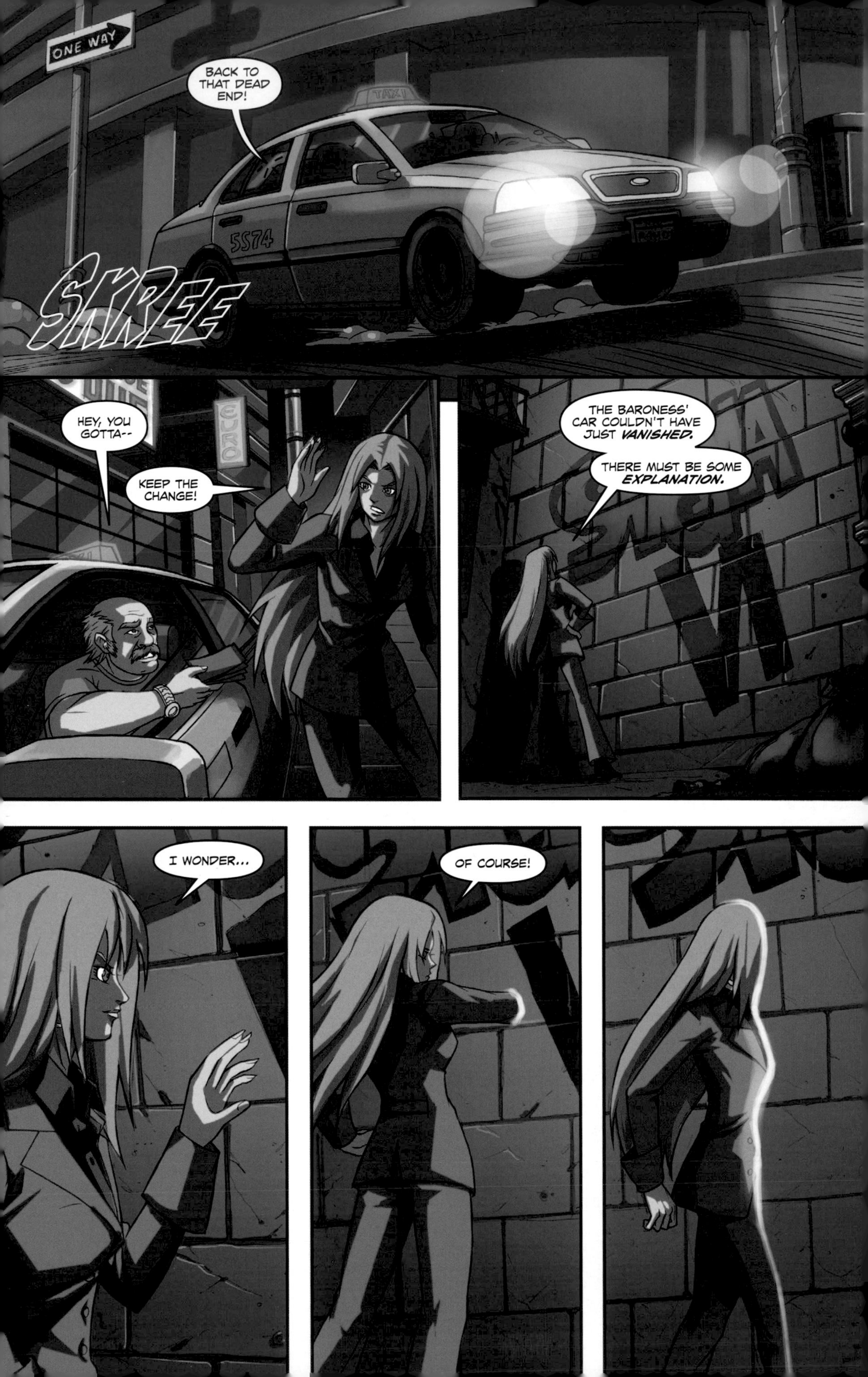
ONE WAY
BACK TO THAT DEAD END!
TAXI
5S74
SKREE
HEY, YOU GOTTA--
KEEP THE CHANGE!
EURO
THE BARONESS' CAR COULDN'T HAVE JUST VANISHED.
THERE MUST BE SOME EXPLANATION.
I WONDER...
OF COURSE!

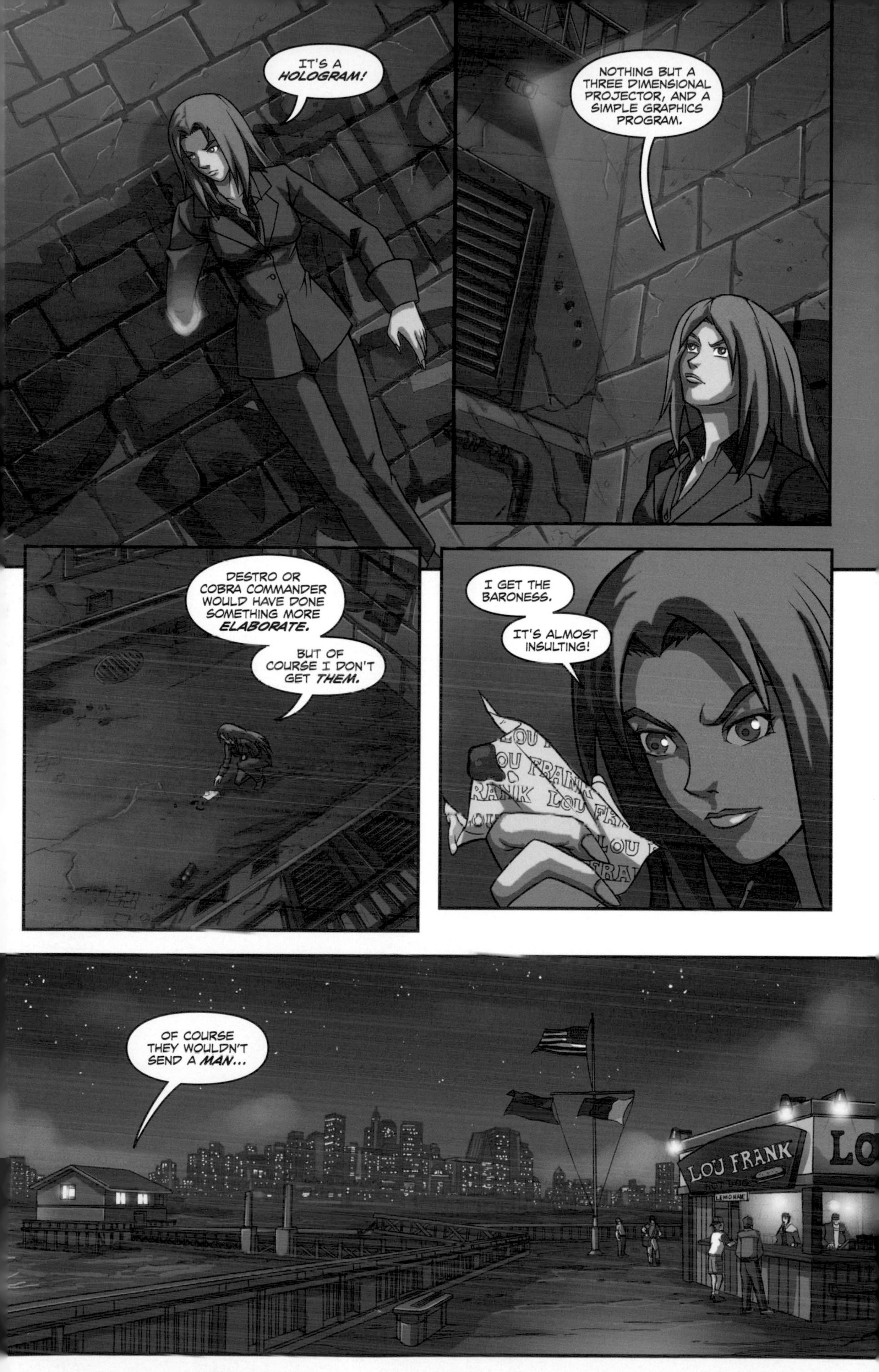
IT'S A HOLOGRAM!
NOTHING BUT A THREE DIMENSIONAL PROJECTOR, AND A SIMPLE GRAPHICS PROGRAM.
DESTRO OR COBRA COMMANDER WOULD HAVE DONE SOMETHING MORE ELABORATE.
BUT OF COURSE I DON'T GET THEM.
I GET THE BARONESS.
IT'S ALMOST INSULTING!
OF COURSE THEY WOULDN'T SEND A MAN...
LOU FRANK
LO
LEMONADE

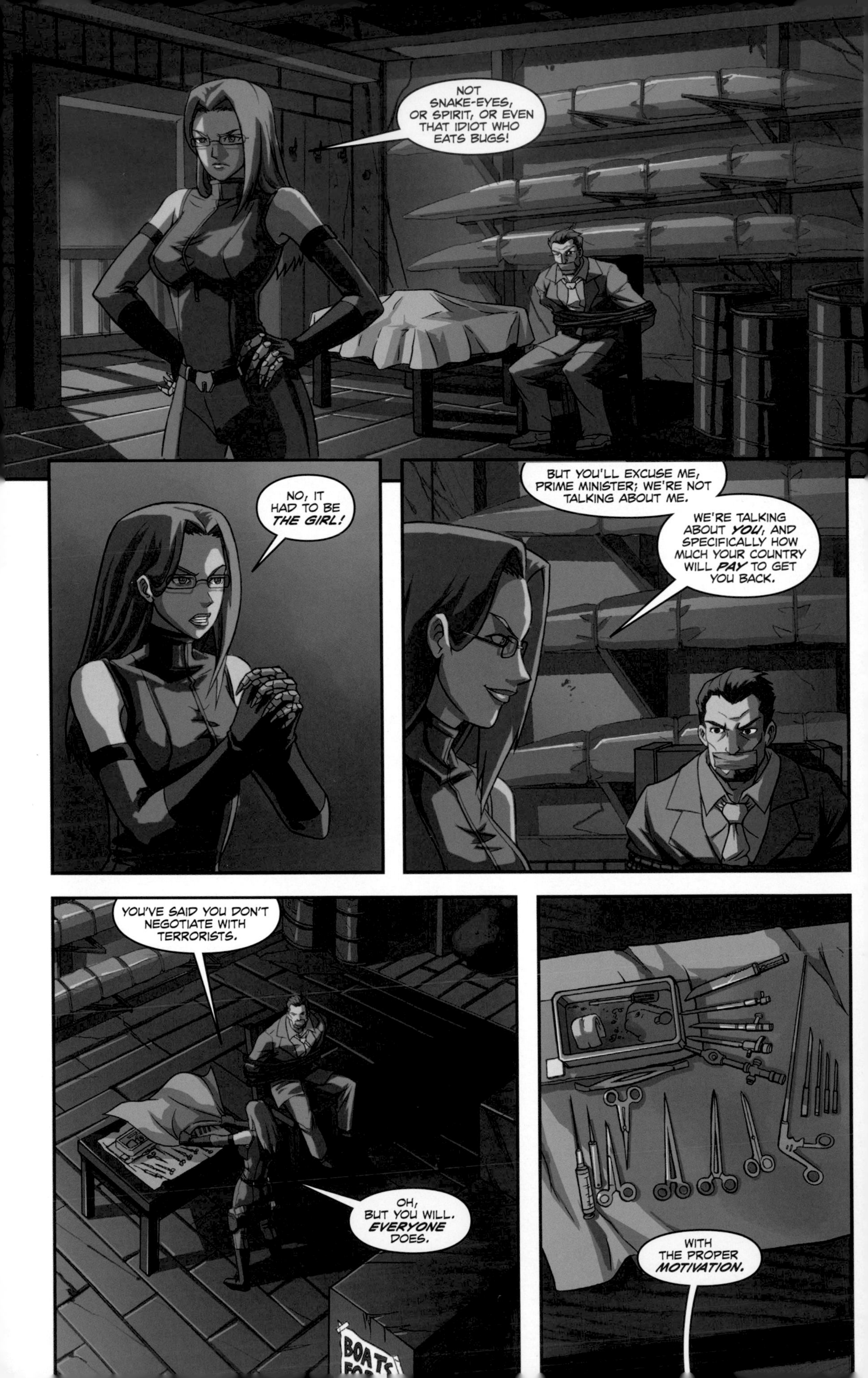
NOT SNAKE-EYES, OR SPIRIT, OR EVEN THAT IDIOT WHO EATS BUGS!
NO, IT HAD TO BE *THE GIRL!*
BUT YOU'LL EXCUSE ME, PRIME MINISTER; WE'RE NOT TALKING ABOUT ME.
WE'RE TALKING ABOUT *YOU*, AND SPECIFICALLY HOW MUCH YOUR COUNTRY WILL *PAY* TO GET YOU BACK.
YOU'VE SAID YOU DON'T NEGOTIATE WITH TERRORISTS.
OH, BUT YOU WILL. *EVERYONE* DOES.
BOATS
WITH THE PROPER *MOTIVATION.*

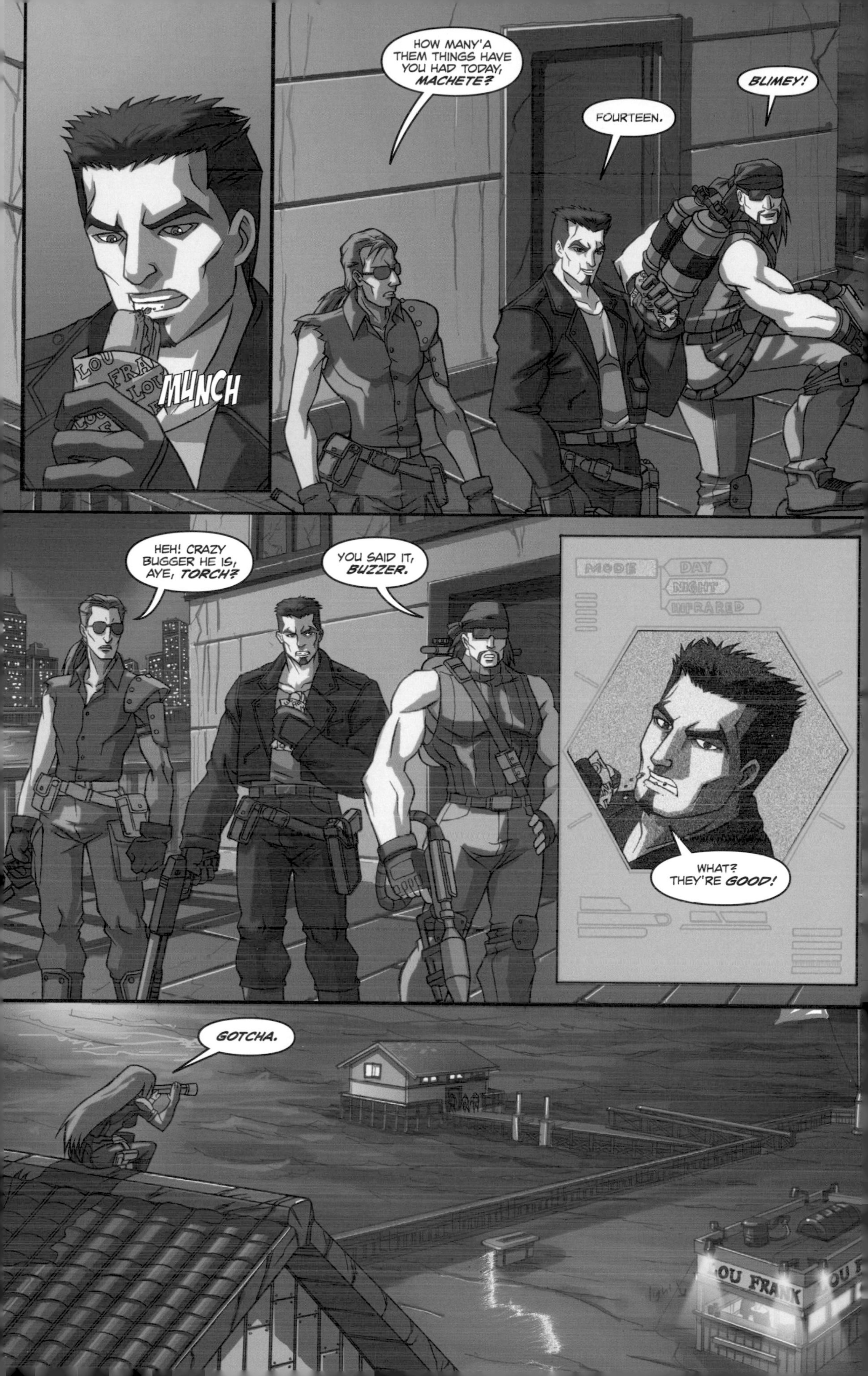
MUNCH
HOW MANY'A THEM THINGS HAVE YOU HAD TODAY, MACHETE?
FOURTEEN.
BLIMEY!
HEH! CRAZY BUGGER HE IS, AYE, TORCH?
YOU SAID IT, BUZZER.
MODE
DAY
NIGHT
INFRARED
WHAT? THEY'RE GOOD!
GOTCHA.
LOU FRANK

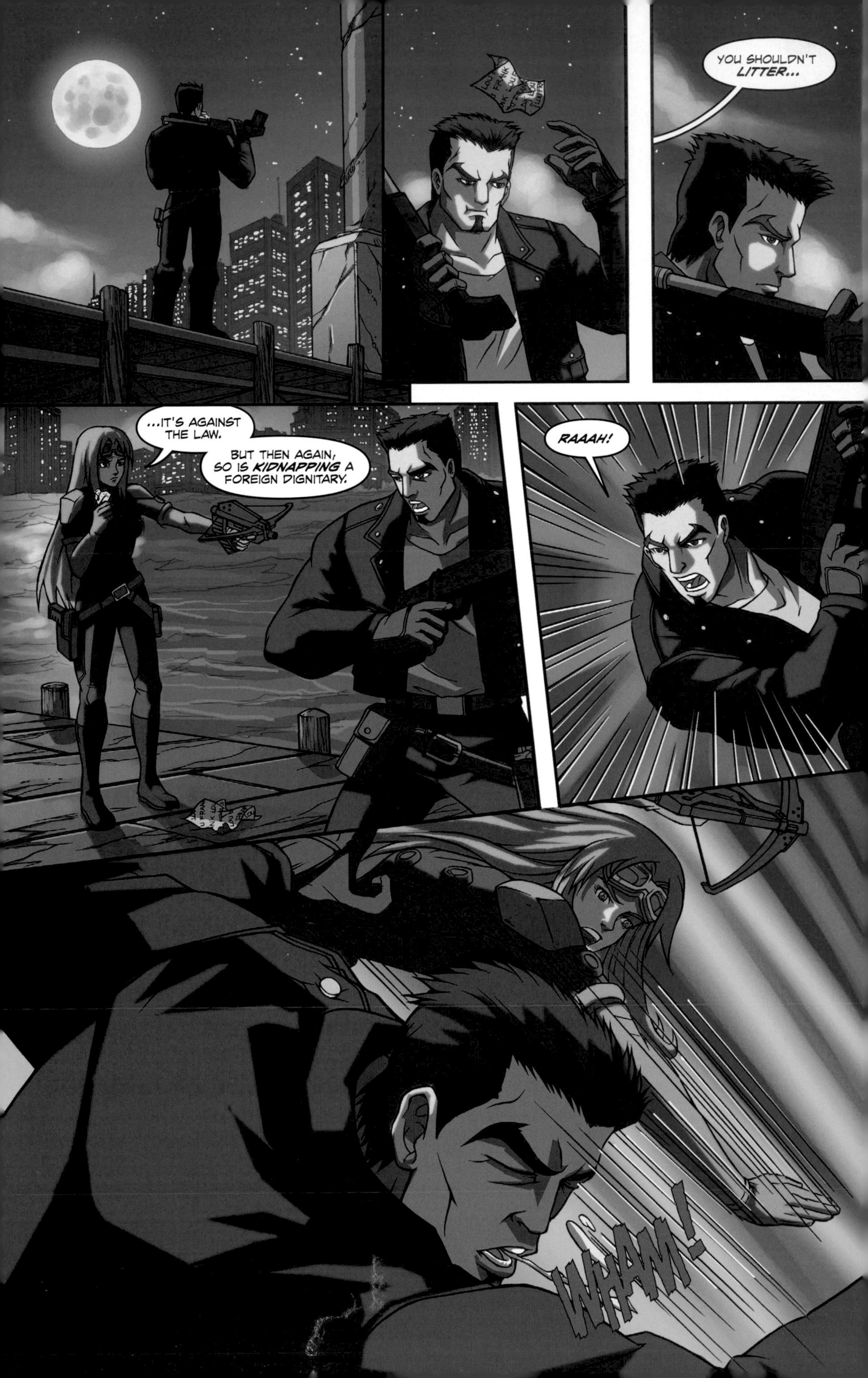
YOU SHOULDN'T LITTER...
...IT'S AGAINST THE LAW.
BUT THEN AGAIN, SO IS KIDNAPPING A FOREIGN DIGNITARY.
RAAAH!
WHAM!

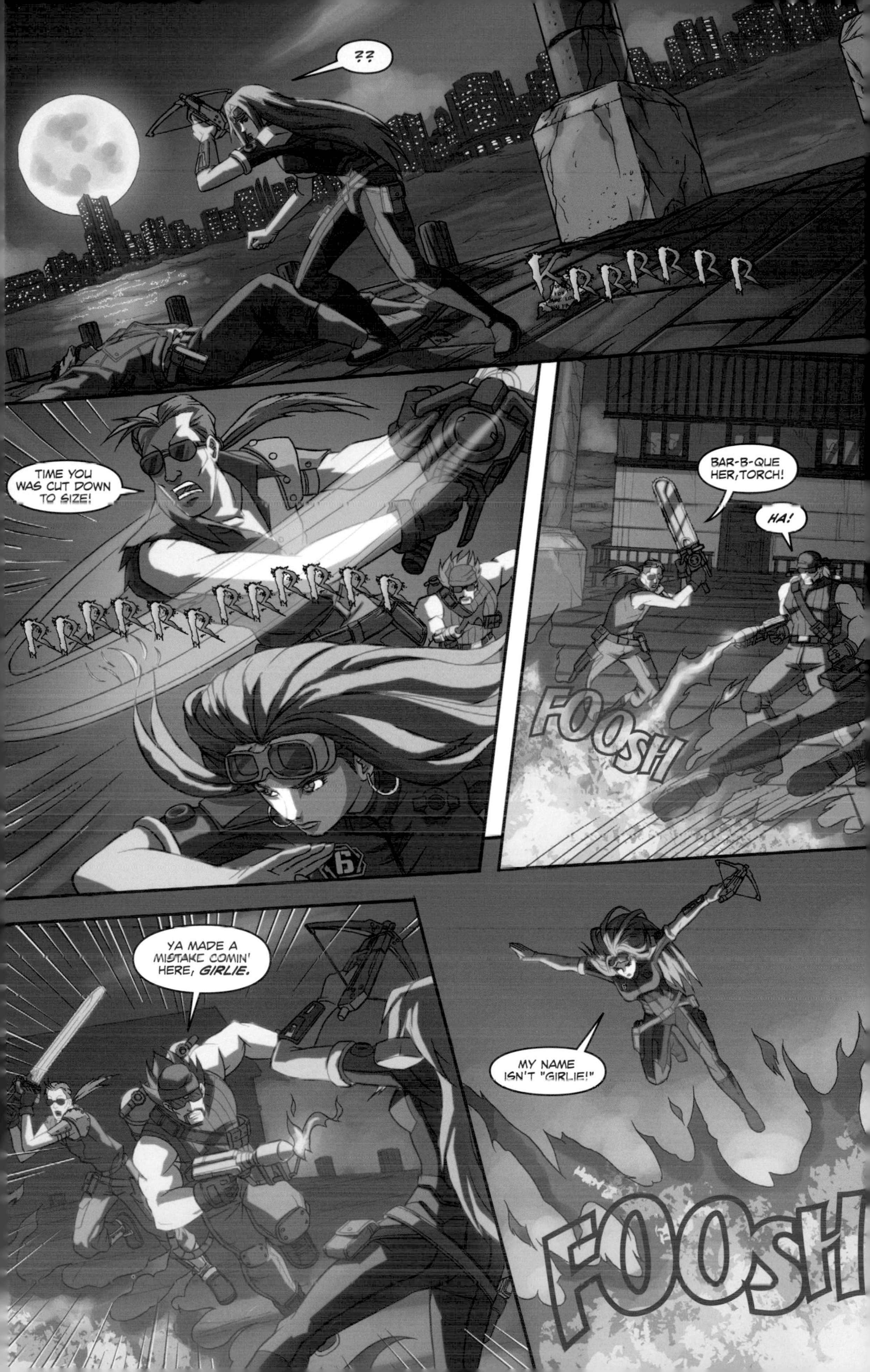
??
KRRRRRR
TIME YOU WAS CUT DOWN TO SIZE!
RRRRRRRRRRRRR
BAR-B-QUE HER, TORCH!
HA!
FOOSH
YA MADE A MISTAKE COMIN' HERE, GIRLIE.
MY NAME ISN'T "GIRLIE!"
FOOSH

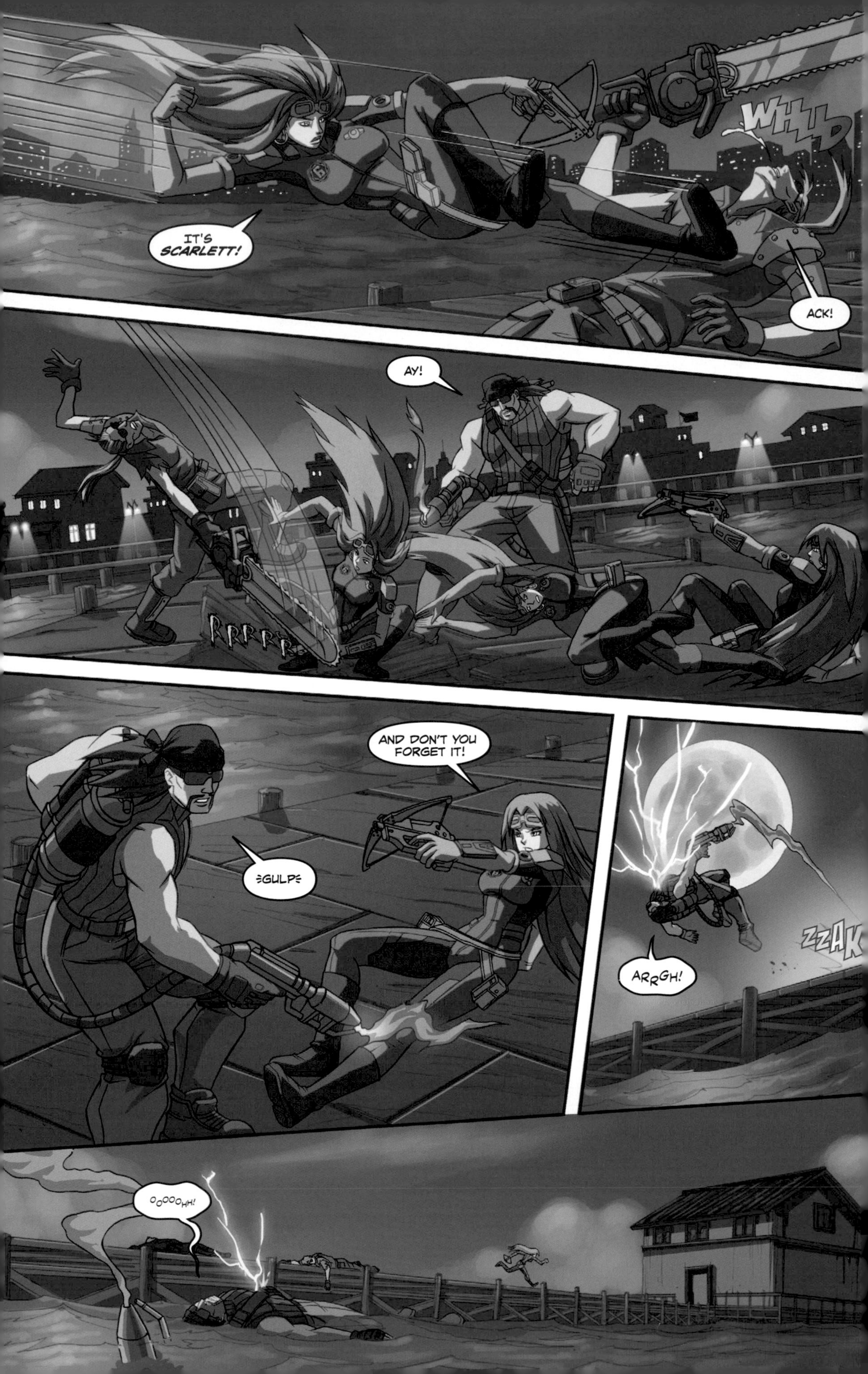

IT'S SCARLETT!
WHUD
ACK!
AY!
RRRRRR
AND DON'T YOU FORGET IT!
GULP
ZZAK
ARRGH!
OOOOOHH!

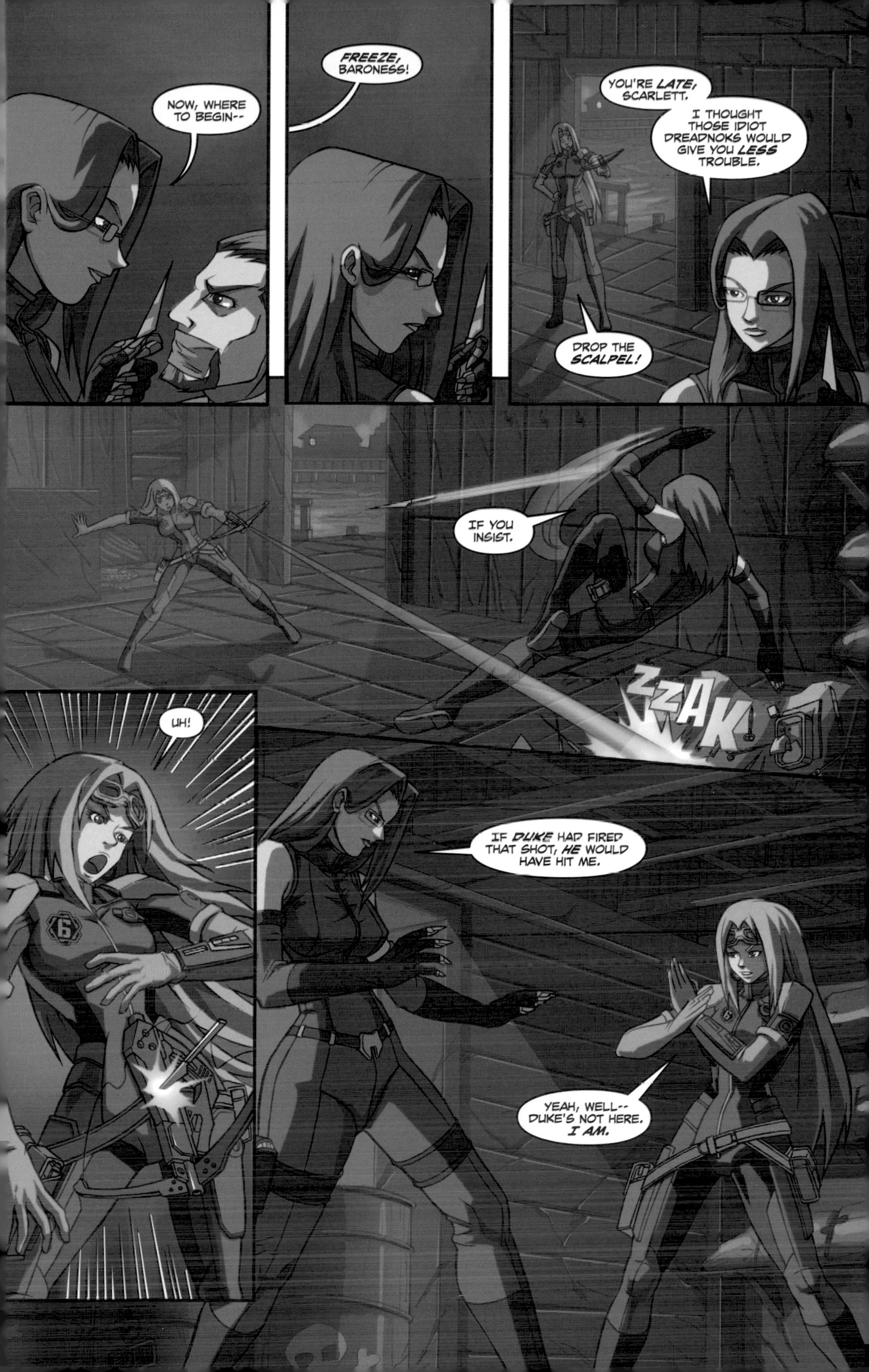
NOW, WHERE TO BEGIN--
FREEZE, BARONESS!
YOU'RE LATE, SCARLETT.
I THOUGHT THOSE IDIOT DREADNOKS WOULD GIVE YOU LESS TROUBLE.
DROP THE SCALPEL!
IF YOU INSIST.
ZZAK!
UH!
IF DUKE HAD FIRED THAT SHOT, HE WOULD HAVE HIT ME.
YEAH, WELL-- DUKE'S NOT HERE. I AM.

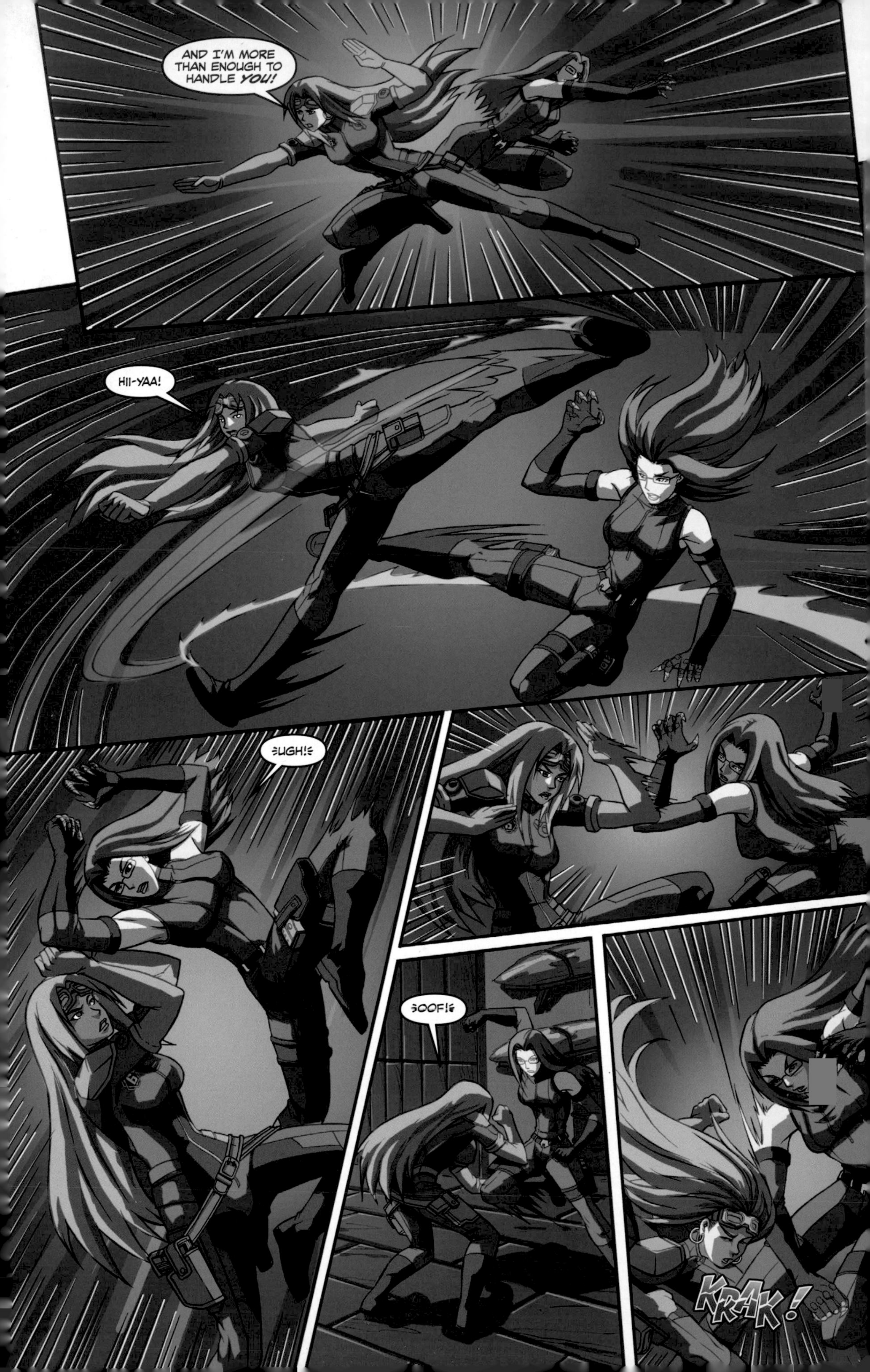
AND I'M MORE THAN ENOUGH TO HANDLE YOU!
HII-YAA!
UGH!
OOF!
KRAK!

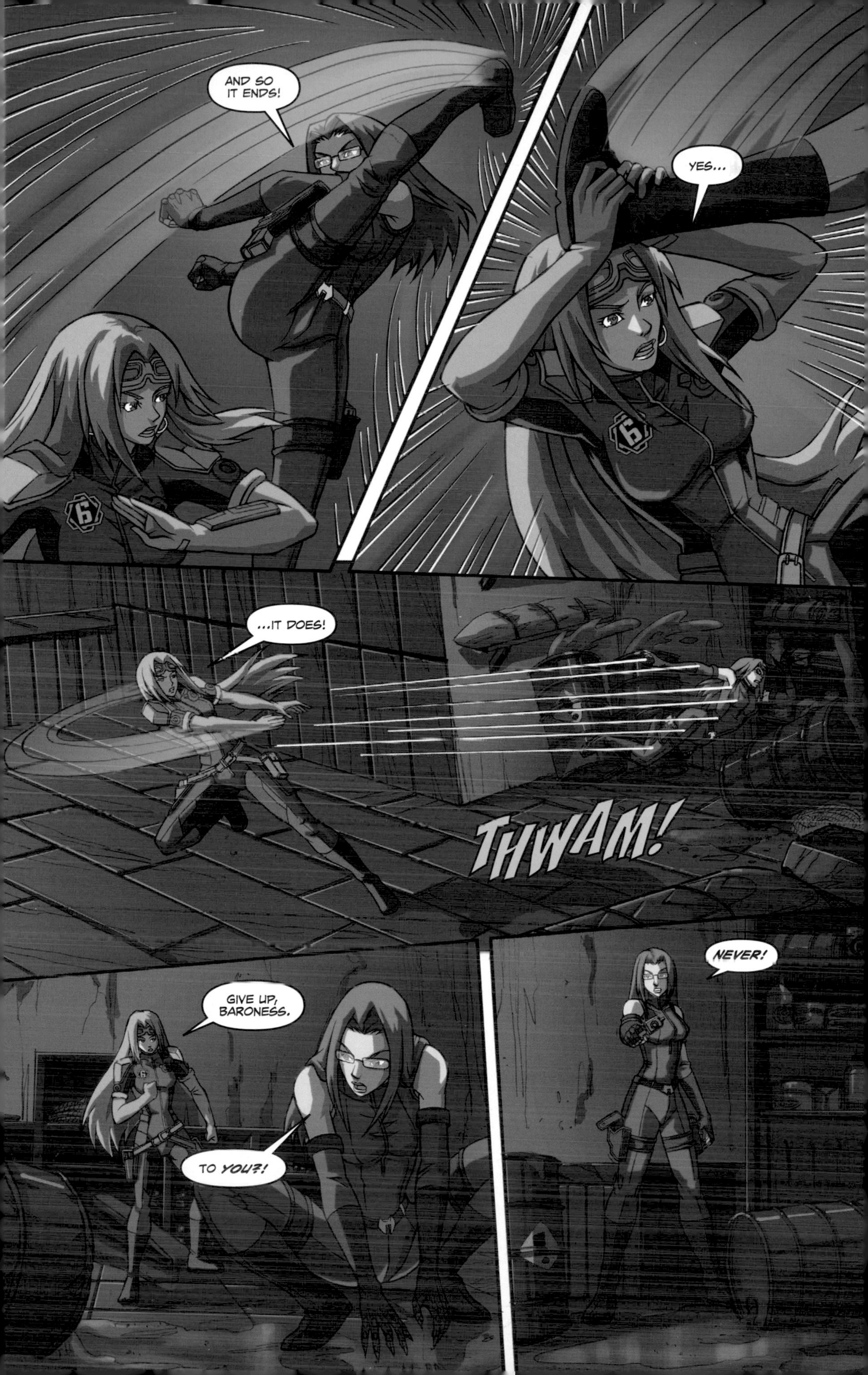
AND SO IT ENDS!
YES...
...IT DOES!
THWAM!
GIVE UP, BARONESS.
TO YOU?!
NEVER!

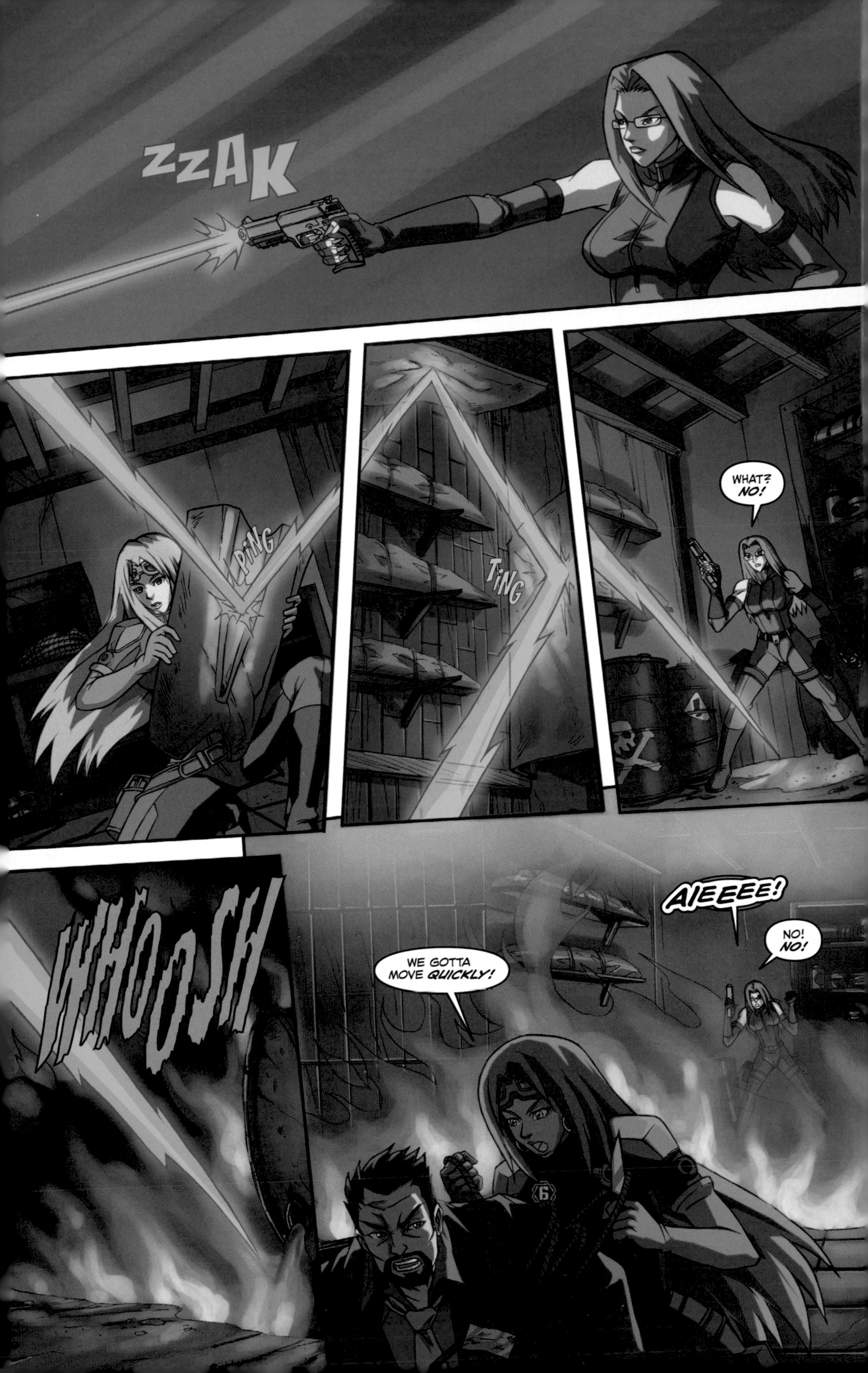
ZZAK
PING
TING
WHAT? NO!
WHOOSH
AIEEEE!
NO! NO!
WE GOTTA MOVE QUICKLY!

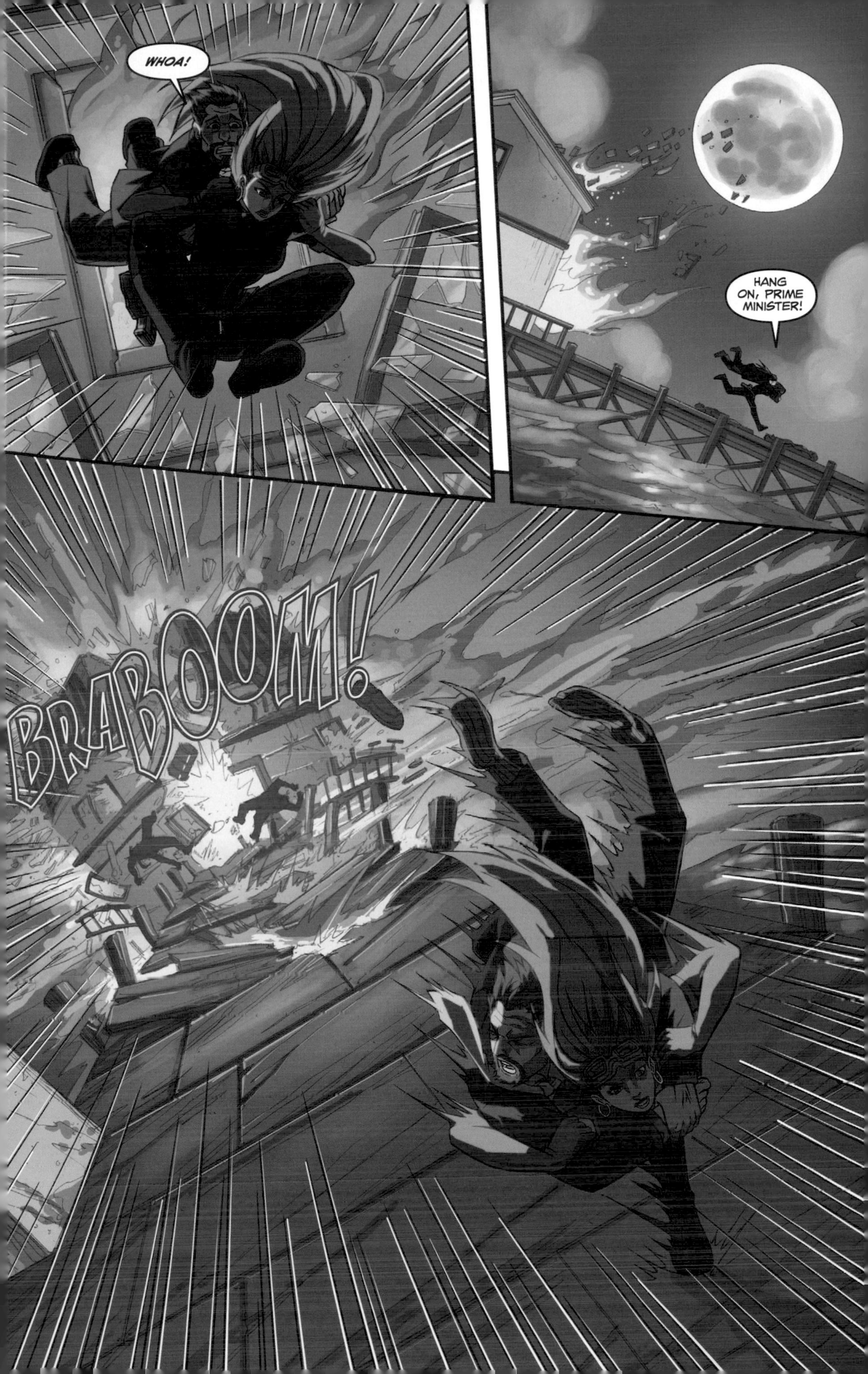
WHOA!
HANG ON, PRIME MINISTER!
BRABOOM!

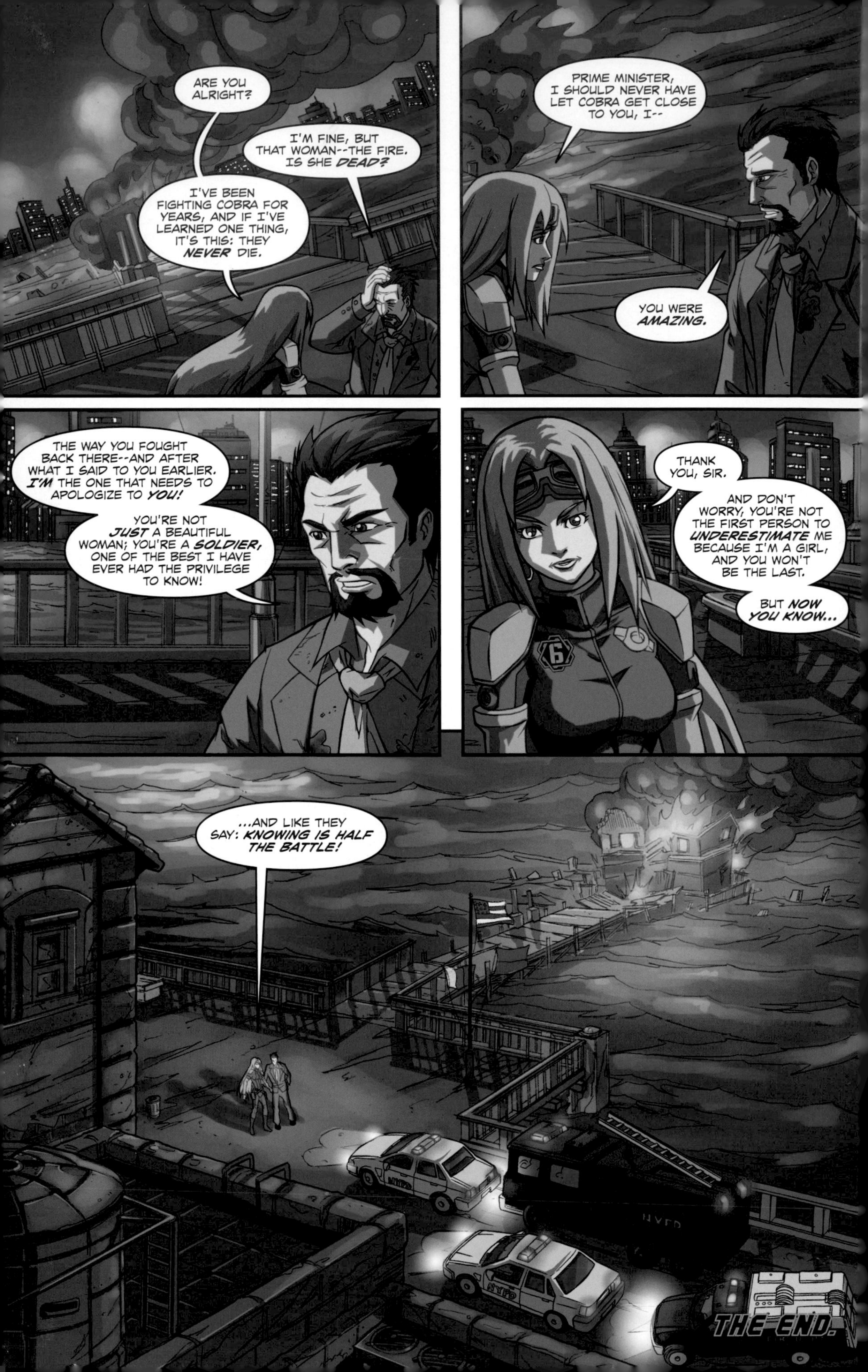
ARE YOU ALRIGHT?
I'M FINE, BUT THAT WOMAN--THE FIRE. IS SHE DEAD?
I'VE BEEN FIGHTING COBRA FOR YEARS, AND IF I'VE LEARNED ONE THING, IT'S THIS: THEY NEVER DIE.
PRIME MINISTER, I SHOULD NEVER HAVE LET COBRA GET CLOSE TO YOU, I--
YOU WERE AMAZING.
THE WAY YOU FOUGHT BACK THERE--AND AFTER WHAT I SAID TO YOU EARLIER. I'M THE ONE THAT NEEDS TO APOLOGIZE TO YOU!
YOU'RE NOT JUST A BEAUTIFUL WOMAN; YOU'RE A SOLDIER, ONE OF THE BEST I HAVE EVER HAD THE PRIVILEGE TO KNOW!
THANK YOU, SIR.
AND DON'T WORRY, YOU'RE NOT THE FIRST PERSON TO UNDERESTIMATE ME BECAUSE I'M A GIRL, AND YOU WON'T BE THE LAST.
BUT NOW YOU KNOW...
...AND LIKE THEY SAY: KNOWING IS HALF THE BATTLE!
NYFD
NYPD
THE END.